P9-DDL-880

For my father, Irving Schwartz, heartfelt son of
New Waterford, who said, We owe everything
to the miners. — JS

For my father and my son. — SS

Text copyright © 2017 by Joanne Schwartz
Illustrations copyright © 2017 by Sydney Smith
Published in Canada and the USA in 2017 by Groundwood Books
Second printing 2017

All rights reserved. No part of this publication may be reproduced, stored in a retrieval
system or transmitted, in any form or by any means, without the prior written consent of
the publisher or a license from The Canadian Copyright
Licensing Agency (Access Copyright). For an Access Copyright license,
visit www.accesscopyright.ca or call toll free to 1-800-893-5777.

Groundwood Books / House of Anansi Press
groundwoodbooks.com

We acknowledge for their financial support of our publishing program the Canada
Council for the Arts, the Ontario Arts Council and the Government of Canada.

Library and Archives Canada Cataloguing in Publication
Schwartz, Joanne (Joanne F.), author
Town is by the sea / Joanne Schwartz ; illustrated by Sydney Smith.
Issued in print and electronic formats.
ISBN 978-1-55498-871-6 (hardback). — ISBN 978-1-55498-872-3 (pdf)
I. Smith, Sydney, illustrator II. Title.
PS8637.C592T69 2017   jC813'.6   C2016-905749-6
C2016-905750-X

The illustrations were done in ink, watercolor and a bit of gouache.
Design by Michael Solomon
Printed and bound in Malaysia

  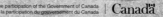 

Canada Council   Conseil des Arts
for the Arts   du Canada

ONTARIO ARTS COUNCIL
CONSEIL DES ARTS DE L'ONTARIO
an Ontario government agency
un organisme du gouvernement de l'Ontario

With the participation of the Government of Canada
Avec la participation du gouvernement du Canada | Canada

MIX
Paper from
responsible sources
FSC® C012700

Town Is by the Sea

Joanne Schwartz   pictures by Sydney Smith

 GROUNDWOOD BOOKS   HOUSE OF ANANSI PRESS   TORONTO   BERKELEY

R0448776526

From my house, I can see
the sea.

It goes like this — house,
road, grassy cliff, sea.

And town spreads out, this way
and that.

My father is a miner and he works under
the sea, deep down in the coal mines.

When I wake up, it goes like this —

first I hear the seagulls, then I hear a dog barking,
a car goes by on the shore road, someone slams a
door and yells good morning.

And along the road, lupines and Queen Anne's lace
rustle in the wind.

First thing I see when I look
out the window is the sea.

And I know my father is already deep
down under that sea, digging for coal.

When I go out in the morning, it goes like this —

I run out of my house and knock at my
friend's door and we head down to the old
rickety playground.

There are only two swings left now, one for big kids and one for babies. There used to be four. One broke, and the other one is wound so high around the top post it will never come down.

I don't care. I stand in the baby one, and my friend swings on the big one. We go so high butterflies rush through my stomach.

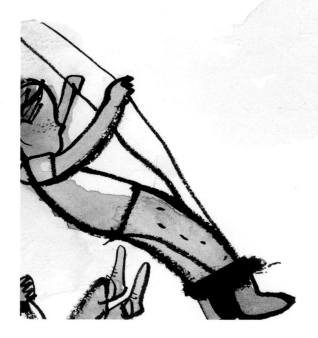

We go so high I can see far out to sea.

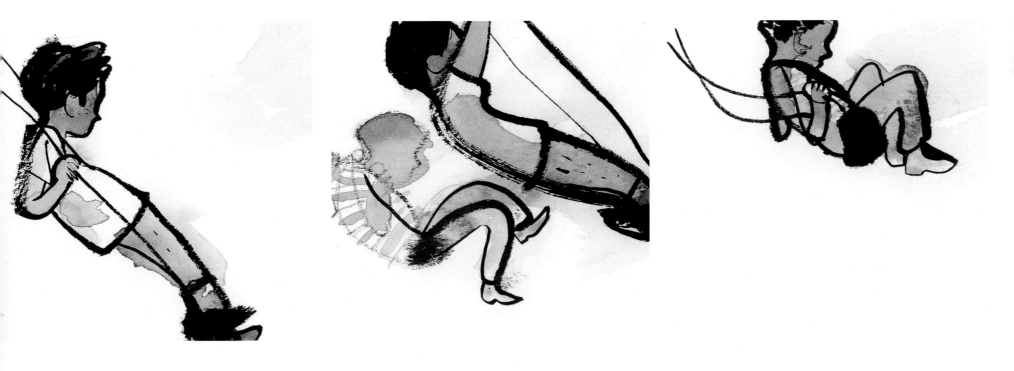

Far out at sea, the waves have white tips.

And deep down under that sea, my father
is digging for coal.

When I get home for lunch, it goes like this —

my mother has a baloney sandwich on the
table and a tall glass of milk. I gulp it down
and eat a big pile of carrots.

My mom says, I need your help now.

She sends me to the store with a list for
the grocer. The store is only a couple of
blocks away on Main Street. The kitchen
door slams on the way out.

Even walking slowly, I get to the store in no time.

It's so sunny today…

the sea is sparkling.

And deep down under that sea, my father
is digging for coal.

In the afternoon, it goes like this —

I go to the graveyard to visit my grandfather, my
father's father. He was a miner, too.
	The air smells like salt. I can taste it on my tongue.

My grandfather used to say,
Bury me facing the sea b'y,
I worked long and hard
underground.

When there are big storms
here, the waves crash against the
shore, battering his gravestone
with salt-soaked spray.

That's okay. My grandfather is
used to storms.

Today the sea is all calm...

and quiet.

And deep down under that sea, my father
is digging for coal.

At supper time, it goes like this —

my father comes home from work. He has black
smudges on his face from working the coal. He looks
tired, but he gives me a big smile and a hug. His long
workday is over, and he is home safe and sound.

He showers and puts on clean clothes and comes down to eat. My mother has been cooking, and the kitchen smells like chicken stew and potatoes.

I listen to the ball game on the radio while I set the table.

After dinner, my mother and father sit on
the porch drinking cups of tea and talking.

The sun sets slowly,

sinking into the sea.

Deep down under that sea is where
my father digs for coal.

At nighttime, it goes like this —

 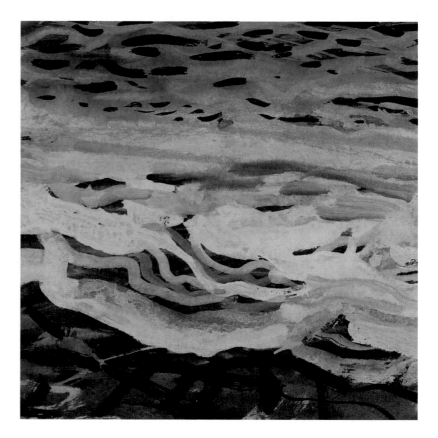

as I fall asleep I can hear the whooshing back and
forth of the waves.
    I think about the sea, and I think about my father.

I think about the bright days of summer

and the dark tunnels underground.
One day, it will be my turn.

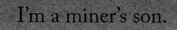

I'm a miner's son.

In my town, that's the way it goes.

Author's Note

"At the centre of the boy's life in coal towns and villages was the mine. He was raised within sight of it; the smell of coal dust was as familiar to him as the sounds of steam pumps and hoists. The boy may have seen for years his father and older brothers leave for the pit. For most boys raised within these communities, the day arrived when they too surrendered their childhood to it."

(From *Boys in the Pits: Child Labour in Coal Mines* by Robert McIntosh)

If you were a boy in the mining towns of Cape Breton — or, indeed, a child in any mining town in the world — during the late 1800s and early 1900s, you might well have faced the prospect of going to work in the mines at the young age of nine or ten, enduring twelve-hour days in the harsh, dangerous and dark reality underground. Decades later, the life of these towns still revolved around the mines. Even into the 1950s, around the time when this story takes place, boys of high-school age, carrying on the traditions of their fathers and grandfathers, continued to see their future working in the mines.

This was the legacy of a mining town.